I'll play the flute.

When I'm big, I'll collect stamps.

I'll go swimming
and I'll jump in, too.

When I'm big, I'll draw pictures.

I'll do gymnastics.

I'll play tennis.

I'll learn judo.

And I'll play
the violin.

When I'm big, I'll be a dancer.

I'll be a gardener.

I'll be a
racing skater.

And I'll read books.
When I'm big,
I'm going to do
lots of things.

BRUNA BOOKS

The little bird
Tilly and Tessa
The fish
The egg
Circus
The king
The sailor
The school
The apple
Pussy Nell
Snuffy
Snuffy and the fire
A story to tell
I am a clown
My vest is white
I can count
I can count more
I can read

I can read more
I can read difficult words
I can dress myself
Miffy
Miffy's birthday
Miffy at the seaside
Miffy in the snow
Miffy at the zoo
Miffy goes flying
Miffy in the hospital
Miffy at the playground
Miffy's Dream
Poppy Pig
Poppy Pig's Garden
Poppy Pig goes to Market
When I'm big
I know about numbers
I know more about numbers

ALSO BY DICK BRUNA

Dick Bruna's ABC Frieze
Dick Bruna's 123 Frieze
Dick Bruna's Animal Frieze
Dick Bruna's Nature Frieze

Dick Bruna's Read-with-Miffy Frieze
The Christmas Book
B is for Bear
Dick Bruna's Animal Book

First published in Great Britain 1981
by Methuen Children's Books Ltd
11 New Fetter Lane, London EC4P 4EE
Reprinted 1981
First published in USA 1981
by Methuen Inc., 733 Third Avenue, New York, NY 10017
Copyright © 1980 Dick Bruna
English text copyright © 1981 Methuen Children's Books Ltd
Illustrations Dick Bruna
Copyright © Mercis bv 1967, 1969, 1974, 1977, 1980
Printed in Great Britain by
Hazell Watson & Viney Ltd, Aylesbury, Bucks
ISBN 0 416 20860 6